In Our Neighborhood

Meet a Coach!

by Cyndy Unwin

Illustrations by Lisa Hunt

Children's Press®
An imprint of Scholastic Inc.

SCHOLASTIC

Special thanks to our content consultant:

Noah Jefferson, Director of the Youth Academy
VBR Star Soccer Club
Roanoke, VA

Library of Congress Cataloging-in-Publication Data
Names: Unwin, Cynthia, author. | Hunt, Lisa, 1973– illustrator.
Title: In our neighborhood. Meet a coach!/by Cyndy Unwin; illustrations by Lisa Hunt.
Other titles: Meet a coach
Description: First edition. | New York: Children's Press, an imprint of Scholastic Inc., 2021. | Series: In our
    neighborhood | Includes index. | Audience: Ages 5–7. | Audience: Grades K–1. | Summary: "This book
    introduces the role of coaches in their community"— Provided by publisher.
Identifiers: LCCN 2021058749 (print) | LCCN 2021058750 (ebook) | ISBN 9781338768824 (library binding) |
    ISBN 9781338768831 (paperback) | ISBN 9781338768848 (ebook)
Subjects: LCSH: Coaches (Athletics)—Juvenile literature. | Coaching (Athletics)—Juvenile literature.
Classification: LCC GV711 .U59 2021 (print) | LCC GV711 (ebook) | DDC 796.07/7—dc23
LC record available at https://lccn.loc.gov/2021058749
LC ebook record available at https://lccn.loc.gov/2021058750

10 9 8 7 6 5 4 3 2 1   22 23 24 25 26

Printed in Heshan, China 62
First edition, 2022

Series produced by Spooky Cheetah Press
Prototype design by Maria Bergós/Book & Look
Page design by Kathleen Petelinsek/The Design Lab

Photos ©: 7: FatCamera/Getty Images; 9: John Jones/Icon Sportswire/Getty
Images; 13: JohnnyGreig/Getty Images; 15: SDI Productions/Getty Images;
16 left: Thomas Barwick/Getty Images; 17 left: Erik Isakson/age fotostock;
17 right: Fuse/Getty Images; 18: Steven M. Falk/TNS/Newscom; 20: andresr/
Getty Images; 22: Fuse/Getty Images; 25: bonniej/Getty Images.

All other photos © Shutterstock.

Table of Contents

OUR NEIGHBORHOOD

Hi! I'm Emma. This is my best friend, Theo. Welcome to our neighborhood!

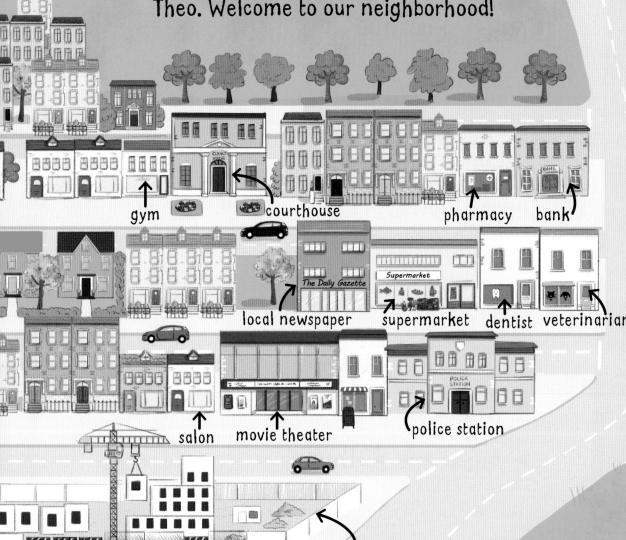

gym

courthouse

pharmacy

bank

local newspaper

supermarket

dentist

veterinarian

salon

movie theater

police station

construction site

recycling center

fire station

EMERGENCY ER

AMBULANCE

hospital

restaurant

Gino's

post office

library

school

CARVER ELEMENTARY SCHOOL

café

There's our school. Both Theo and I love to play soccer at recess. And now we're going to join a real soccer team!

Theo told me about the soccer team at recess last week.
He was very excited. He wanted me to join, too.

I was nervous. I had never played on a team before.

Playing on a sports team has many benefits. Regular exercise is important for good health. Being on a team also teaches you new skills and how to get along with others.

MEET COACH ABBY

My parents brought me to the first team meeting. We met Coach Abby. She told us she had been the captain of her college soccer team.

Coach Abby seemed really nice. But I still wasn't sure about joining the team. My parents encouraged me to try.

Many coaches have experience playing the sport they coach. A person doesn't have to have playing experience to be a good coach, though.

Try it. You might like it!

I guess you're right, Dad!

PRACTICE TIME

At our first practice, Coach Abby taught us soccer rules. Most of us can't touch the ball with our hands while we play. The goalkeeper is the only player who can.

We practiced passing the ball and dribbling. Coach Abby showed us how to kick the ball with the side of our foot. Theo was a really good passer, but it was hard for me.

It just takes practice!

Coaches have to understand the different positions and rules of their sport. They are good teachers who help their players understand their sport.

At our second practice, Coach Abby taught us all the different soccer positions. She said it was important to spread out on the field and not hog the ball.

After practice, we got our team shirts. Theo's number was 6, and mine was 3. Getting the shirt made me excited to be part of a team!

Many sports have offensive and defensive players. Offensive players score the points. Defensive players try to keep the other team from scoring.

We had our first scrimmage, or practice game, at the next practice. Coach Abby told me to play defense, but it didn't seem like anyone was playing the right positions. They all just chased after the ball!

A player ran into me and I fell on my wrist. Coach Abby made sure I wasn't badly hurt. Then she gave me an ice pack for my wrist.

Coaches are trained in first aid, in case players get hurt or sick while playing.

Does it still hurt a lot?

No. It's feeling better now.

After practice, Theo and I asked Coach Abby what other sports she coaches. "I'm focused on soccer," she told us. "But I have friends who coach other sports."

Gymnastics coaches teach kids how to safely perform different moves. Coaches also spot the gymnasts—or support them with their hands—until the gymnasts learn a skill.

Swimming coaches teach kids how to use their arms and legs for the different strokes. Coaches train the swimmers to become faster and stronger.

Baseball and softball coaches teach the players how to play offense and defense. That means teaching the players how to hit the ball and how to catch and throw it.

Basketball coaches also teach offense and defense. They show players how to shoot the ball properly, as well as how to dribble, pass, and steal.

It's my favorite sport!

Why did you pick soccer to coach?

GAME DAY!

Saturday was our first real game! Theo and I got ready at my house. We were going to the game together.

I'm kind of nervous.

Even pro athletes get "the jitters" before a game. Some of them have special traditions or rituals (like listening to music) that they do before every game. These help them stay calm or feel confident.

Theo told me he wanted to play offense, like he did in our scrimmage. I wasn't sure what position I wanted. I just hoped I didn't mess up.

Me too!

Coach Abby gave us a pep talk before the game. She told us the most important thing was to have fun, try our best, and be good sports.

Good coaches motivate their players. They get players excited about their sport. Coaches help players believe in themselves.

Then she gave us our positions. She told Theo to play defense. He was not happy. She told me to play offense. That scared me. I'm just a beginner!

I wasn't sure I could play offense. Coach Abby told me to try my best. My teammates tried to pass the ball to me a few times, but the other team always stole it away.

Good coaches know how to help disappointed players. They help players see that a mistake is a good chance to get better.

Finally, I had a chance. Theo passed the ball to me. I kicked the ball toward the net, but I hit it with my toe. The ball jumped up and sailed wide to the left.

Shake it off, Emma. You got this!

It was almost the end of the game. The score was tied. I wasn't sure if I even wanted someone to pass to me! I felt so much pressure.

Then Theo passed the ball to me. Before I even had time to think, I stopped the ball with my foot, lined it up just right, and shot it toward the goal. SCORE!

Great shot, Emma!

Thanks to your awesome pass!

Coaches teach their players to be good sports. That means players don't brag when they do well—and they don't sulk when they lose.

We celebrated with ice cream after the game.
Coach Abby invited the other team to join us.
"You were great sports!" she told them.

Theo and I decided that being on a soccer team is fun, no matter what position we play. We can't wait for our next game!

Ask a Coach

Theo asked Coach Abby some questions at the end of the day.

What's your favorite part of coaching?

I love seeing kids improve their skills and have fun at the same time.

Do you need special training to be a coach?

Yes and no. Coaches aren't required to have much training. But most take special classes to learn all they can about their sport and how to be a good coach.

What are some ways coaches keep kids safe?

Coaches use safe equipment and they encourage their players to follow the rules. They make sure kids drink enough water, and they keep an eye on the weather in case there is lightning close by.

What makes a great coach?

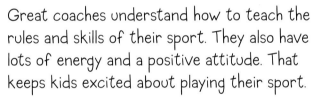

Great coaches understand how to teach the rules and skills of their sport. They also have lots of energy and a positive attitude. That keeps kids excited about playing their sport.

Who can be a coach?

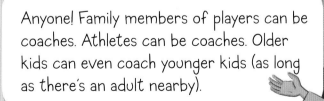

Anyone! Family members of players can be coaches. Athletes can be coaches. Older kids can even coach younger kids (as long as there's an adult nearby).

Coach Abby's Tips for Being a Good Sport

- Have fun! Play fair and don't cheat.

- Support your teammates, even when they make a mistake.

- When you goof up, practice some more and try again.

- Always show respect to your coach, your teammates, the officials, and the other team.

- When your team loses, congratulate the winning team.

- Remember: Disappointment is a chance to learn and grow.

A Coach's Tools

Equipment: A coach has the right equipment for the sport—like a soccer ball!

Whistle: A coach uses a whistle to get the team's attention quickly.

First aid kit: A coach has a first aid kit on hand for players who get bumps and bruises.

Cones: A coach uses cones to set up practice drills.

Index

About the Author

Cyndy Unwin lives in the mountains of Virginia with her husband and very nonathletic cat, Max. She met many great coaches when her daughters competed in gymnastics, dance, and volleyball.